Y0-BVR-524

Noel Olson
Cheers!

fleabite

"For all well-hugged stuffed toys"

Illustrations and Text Copyright ©2004 by Noel Olson
First Edition
Published by Terra Linda Publishing
Manufactured in Korea
ISBN: 0-9746710-0-2 (hardcover)

All rights reserved. No part of this book may be reproduced or transmitted in any form by any means, electronic, mechanical, photocopying, recording, or otherwise, without prior permission of the publisher.

Terra Linda Publishing, www.terralindapublishing.com, San Rafael, California

fleabite

by

noel e. olson

fleabite
is
my
very
FLAT
dog

"His stuffing is as flat as a pancake!"

He can float on the breeze
like a frisbee

pretend he's a

curtain in the kitchen

Alice in Wonderland
KAFKA
Aesops
Dick and Jane
ABC's
Lassie
Snoopy
BEOWÖLF

And

hide in my bookshelf

leabite can fly
like a kite

And likes to hide under the rug

"HAng ten!"

YAY

Sometimes

fleabite goes surfing in the ocean
and all the fish
clap and cheer!

If he licked a stamp
and
wore it

.37

to: MOM
123 dogbone Lane

You might think he was a letter

We play
Hide-n-Seek
in the forest,

In my garden,

And under my bed

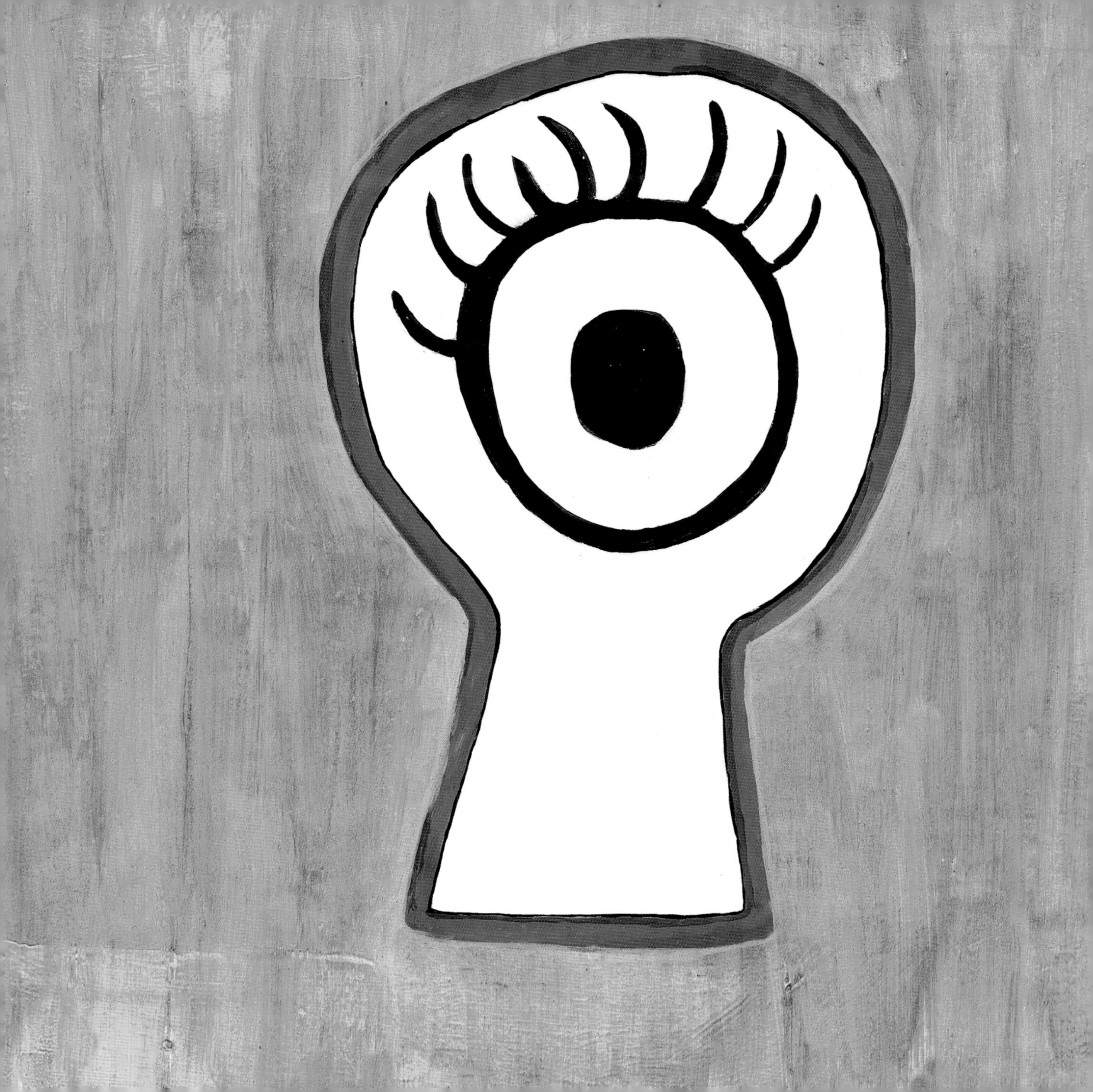

But

best of all, fleabite sneaks through the crack in my door at night

and is my
extra blanket

"night, night!"
Love, fleabite